TEDDY BEAR MURDER

Frosted Love Cozy Mysteries, Book 8

SUMMER PRESCOTT

The Story Behind The Story

Sometimes looking back is painful. Just when I had begun to become more confident about the Cozy genre, three years ago, I was devastated by the reviews on this book. Prior reviews had brought up good points, and I had learned a ton from reader commentary, but the critical reviews on this one were profoundly negative, and a little bit personal. Thankfully, I was too busy writing at this point to be able to pay much attention to them.

I was producing a book per week, which is part of the reason why the books were so short. They're meant to be like TV episodes, where the reader could "tune in" each week for a visit with their literary friends. In order to write a book a week, I'd write for between 5-6 hours per day, three days a week, and take the rest of the week off. I loved this schedule and loved being able to write for a living. It was around this time that I wondered how long the series would last, or if I'd run out of ideas. I'd always thought that writing a book meant writing one standalone book and then moving on to the next, so I found the idea of having to continue a series with the same characters to be a bit of a challenge. I hadn't fully gotten to 'know' my characters yet, but I was getting more of a grasp on them with each book. If someone had told me back then that I'd write 62 books (and counting) with the same characters, I'd have laughed, but such is the case, and with every Missy and Chas book, I grow to love them, their family and friends even more.

Thank you, dear readers, for sticking with me through thick and thin, and giving me the encouragement that I needed when the road ahead got really rocky. I couldn't have made it without you!

Chapter 1

Melissa Gladstone hurried into her Dellville, Louisiana cupcake shop, Crème de la Cupcake, pulling her coat tightly around her. The morning was chilly, and the wind sliced through her light jacket and whipped her blonde curls about in a manner that brought visions of snowflakes to mind. She was a tousled mess when she closed the front door firmly behind her, but smiled at her store manager, Cheryl, upon her arrival. She had just gotten engaged last week to the bright young graduate student, Ben, who managed Missy's other store in the neighboring town of LaChance, and Missy couldn't be happier.

Cheryl was in the midst of the morning rush, so Missy shed her coat in the back room, rolled up her sleeves and went right to work. She began by helping out Cheryl and her assistant Grayson with the sizable line of people waiting to grab cupcakes, along with their morning coffee. When the rush died down to a manageable line, Missy slipped back to the kitchen to put together the to-go orders that would need to be delivered during the day to various businesses and events.

She had just packaged up four dozen strawberry cupcakes for a baby shower, when Grayson appeared at the kitchen doorway.

"Phone for you Ms. G.," he announced. "It's Ben."

"Are you sure it's for me and not Cheryl?" she grinned, teasing.

Grayson chuckled. "For once, it's not."

He headed back to the front counter and Missy picked up the extension in her tiny office, off of the kitchen. "Good morning, lovely groom-to-be," she sang out. "What can I do for you today?"

She could almost hear the blush in Ben's voice when he replied. "Hi, Ms. G., I just wanted to let you know that I got a call from Mrs. Christianson at the Women's Auxiliary. They're having some sort of charity event and she wants to talk to you about volunteering and making a donation. I have her number here if you want to call her back."

Missy sighed inwardly. She wasn't a member of the Auxiliary, but she tried to help out many of the local charities in her home town of LaChance, and community leaders knew that she was dependable in a pinch. She hoped that whatever Loretta Christianson needed wouldn't take too up too much time. The weeks between Thanksgiving and Christmas were her busiest of the year, and she hated to turn down an opportunity to help out. Loretta was from one of LaChance's finest families, and had married a local attorney, Sidney Christianson, which merely underscored her already prominent position on the society pages. Far from being a decorative socialite, however, Loretta worked long hours for worthy causes all over the area, and Missy knew that if she was spearheading an event, it would probably pull at her heart strings significantly enough to prompt her to help out.

Her sense of civic duty won out and she dialed the number that Ben had given her.

"Hi, Loretta, it's Missy Gladstone. Ben said that you called," she explained, when the busy organizer picked up the phone.

"Melissa! It's so great to hear from you," Loretta trilled, excitement and relief evident in her voice. "Listen, sugar, I know that it's last minute, but I'm in a bind and I'm hoping that you can help me out. I'm hosting a children's party to benefit the pediatric wing at the hospital, and I just got a call from the caterer. They can do the food for the kiddos, but they don't do desserts, and I'm really hoping that you'll be able to come up with something for me. I can pay you from the slush fund at the Auxiliary."

"Don't be silly, I'll donate whatever cupcakes that you'll need. Ben and I can decorate them to look like clowns and animals and all sorts of fun "kiddie" things," Missy assured her. "When do you need them?" she asked, jotting down notes on a scratch pad.

"Well, see…that's the thing," Loretta sighed. "The event is on Saturday."

"Saturday?" Missy repeated, eyebrows raised. "As in the day after tomorrow?"

"Yes, I'm so sorry, Melissa. You know that I wouldn't ask if it wasn't important. This money is so desperately needed…" she apologized.

"No worries, Loretta, it's okay. I'll have Ben stay late with me tomorrow night to get the baking and decorating done. We'll make it happen. How many guests are you expecting?"

"Oh, thank you, girl, you're the best!" she gushed. "The guests are going to be the children of several of our donors, children of the hospital staff and many of our doctors, and some former patients from the pediatric wing as well. We're looking at probably close to a hundred kids between the ages of 3 and 10."

Missy pursed her lips and swallowed before replying. That many kids translated into multiple large batches of cupcakes. She and Ben would be busy working long hours for the next couple of days, beginning tonight. "Okay, gotcha. I'll make sure that there are no nuts, strawberries, or any other well-known allergens, and we'll bake some vegan and gluten-free choices as well."

"That will be great, thank you so much!" Loretta exclaimed, happy to have another item off of her to-do list.

"No problem, it'll be my pleasure," Missy replied.

"Great! Oh...and Melissa? There's just one more thing..."

Missy's "I'm about to be asked to do something that I probably won't want to do" radar was pinging madly. "Yes, what is it?" she asked, wishing that she had hung up after Loretta thanked her.

"Because of the sheer number of children involved, we don't have enough volunteers to help with the party. Do you think, since you're going to be there setting up the cupcakes anyway, that you might be able to stay and help with crowd control?" she asked hopefully.

Missy bit her lower lip, indecisive. "Loretta...I really don't know the first thing about dealing with children," she confessed. "I've never even babysat."

"Oh, sugar, you'll be a natural, I just know it. You don't have to have any special skills, you can just circulate, make sure the kiddos stay involved and that no one wanders off alone. It's really easy and the other volunteers can bring you up to speed on what needs to happen," she reassured her.

"I don't know..." Missy hesitated, terrified at the thought of being responsible for a roomful of other people's children.

"You'll be great, girl, don't worry about it. I really need you Melissa...please?" Loretta played upon Missy's tender heart.

"Okay," she agreed finally, feeling more than a bit of trepidation.

"Yay! Okay darlin, I've gotta run, but I'll send you an email with all the specifics. Thanks again!" she sang out, hanging up before Missy could change her mind.

As usual, when dealing with the effervescent Loretta Christianson, Missy felt a bit steamrolled, but flattered to have been asked to participate. She pressed the End button on her phone, then dialed Ben to make certain that the groom-to-be had time to help her.

* * *

"I feel like I've been frosting cupcakes forever," Ben remarked, putting the finishing touches on a batch of chocolate cupcakes that looked like teddy bears.

"Me too," Missy agreed, surveying the colorful varieties of

cupcakes lining the counters of the commercial kitchen. "It'll be worth it though, when we see the sweet smiles on the faces of those kids."

Ben looked at her boss with mild concern. "Uhh...yeah. Ms. G., have you ever actually been to a children's party?" he asked.

"Not since I was a child," Missy joked, winking.

"I think it might be a little bit different from what you're envisioning. I've done a lot of babysitting, and quite honestly, sometimes just two or three kids can cause enough commotion to have me wanting to tear my hair out. I can't even imagine dealing with a hundred of them," he warned gently.

"Oh, Ben, honey, how bad could it be? It'll be a bunch of happy kids at a party, playing games and eating treats. It should be one of the happiest situations ever," his boss replied, entirely naïve. "Are you going to stay and help?"

"No," Ben replied quickly and firmly. "I mean, umm...I have, like, some school stuff to work on and...other stuff too," he hedged. "Want me to start boxing these up?"

"Sure, that'll be great," Missy nodded, so involved with her fantasy of a happy party that she didn't notice Ben's obvious aversion to the idea.

It was a kids' party...how bad could it be?

Chapter 2

Saturday morning dawned bright and sunny, and Missy enlisted the help of her beau, tall-dark-and-handsome, Detective Chas Beckett, to help deliver the colorful, kid-themed cupcakes to the grand ballroom of one of LaChance's finest hotels. When she asked if he could stay and help out, the detective replied with a long, non-specific excuse and skedaddled as soon as possible. Missy giggled at the thought of the strong, clever detective being frightened at the prospect of a children's party and thought that he and Ben were being just silly. Children were fun, happy creatures…what could go wrong?

Loretta caught up with Missy as she finished setting up the cupcake table, and, after an appreciative hug, gave her a list of instructions.

"Okay, sugar, here's what you need to do. Make sure that the kids don't come up and grab the cupcakes. Also make sure that when you give one to a child, that no one else takes it away from them or bites it while they're holding it…"

"They would do that?" Missy interrupted, astonished.

"In a heartbeat, darlin," Loretta replied. "The kids with special dietary needs will have color-coded wristbands on – you'll need to review the list that tells you what each color means. Don't let them talk you into giving them something that's not approved."

Missy fidgeted, beginning to get very nervous. "Why on earth would they ask for something that could make them sick?" she wondered.

"Because they're kids," Loretta waved dismissively. "And most likely, the ones who'll try to pull a fast one on you won't ask, they'll scream, cry and demand. Don't worry about it, just politely but firmly say no, and they'll get over it."

Missy blinked at the thought of a child screaming at her, feeling entirely unprepared for what she might be facing.

Loretta saw the look of terror growing in her eyes and patted her arm reassuringly. "You'll be fine, sugar. You're sweet and helpful, and I'm sure the kids are going to love you. It'll be fun, really," she smiled, dashing away before Missy could object.

Half an hour into the party, Missy was exhausted. Trying to hand out cupcakes one at a time, while making sure that no one touched anything on her table and no one was served the wrong type of cupcake for their dietary needs was beyond taxing. No one had happened to mention the effect that sugar can have on some children, and she found herself, mouth agape, watching in amazement as the activity and noise level skyrocketed. Kids ran and shouted, some smiling, some crying, some overwhelmed by the bustle of it all. She had just warned, "No, no, don't touch that, sweetie," for the hundredth time, when Loretta flitted over to her table, seemingly in a panic.

"Oh, Melissa, I don't know what I'm going to do," she fretted.

Seeing the typically calm, cool and in-control organizer in a panic was a surprise. "What's wrong? Can I help you with something?" Missy asked, hoping for an excuse that would take her to a remote location.

"I don't know. We had a magician scheduled to come out, but his car broke down and there's no way that he'll be able to get here in time. I have no idea how I'm going to keep all these children entertained without him," Loretta fretted.

Missy thought for a moment, then snapped her fingers. "I might be able to help. My manager, Ben, volunteers as a clown for parades and at hospitals and charities. He makes balloon animals and the kids absolutely love him. I can see if he's available to come down and help, if you'd like," she offered.

"Oh, Melissa, you are a treasure! Yes, please call him and see what you can do. I owe you for this," Loretta breathed a sigh of relief.

"Not at all, it's for the kids," Missy smiled, glancing around at the impending bedlam.

Ben arrived fifteen minutes later, decked out in a puffy green and purple clown suit with giant red shoes, white gloves, and an oversized head mask. Missy was delighted at the outfit, remarking that she wouldn't have recognized him if she hadn't known who was beneath the mask. He went to work immediately, commanding the attention of the rambunctious tots with jokes, balloons and songs. Missy's heart swelled with pride as she witnessed the good-hearted young man work his magic, literally and figuratively. He entertained for about an hour, the children paying rapt attention and settling down on the floor in a semi-circle around him. Loretta suggested that he take a break, knowing how tiring carrying around the large, papier-mâché head on his shoulders could be, and he nodded gratefully, heading for a back room after snagging a teddy bear cupcake.

Missy looked at her watch when the number of kids crying, and wandering around, bored, seemed to increase significantly. She realized that Ben had been on break for nearly twenty minutes, which was most unusual for the diligent young man. Recruiting one of the adult volunteers to watch the cupcake table, she headed for the break room to remind Ben that he was needed. She entered the room that smelled delightfully of coffee and saw Ben leaning back in a chair, his heavy clown head still on, apparently fast asleep. Suppressing a giggle at the sight of the sleeping clown, she went over and gave his shoulder a squeeze to wake him.

"Hey Bozo, I know you're tired, but we need you out there," she grinned. Shaking him a bit she was concerned when he didn't respond. "Ben? Ben, wake up."

Loretta appeared in the doorway. "Melissa? Is everything okay? I heard your voice…" she trailed off, seeing Missy trying to rouse the clown.

"Ben, I'm going to take your mask off, okay?" she asked the unresponsive young man. Lifting the heavy head from his shoulders, she was astonished to see that the man in the costume wasn't Ben. She looked at Loretta, not knowing what to do.

"I don't know who this is, do you?" she asked, a tickle of fear shooting through her.

"No, I don't. Is he okay?" the worried organizer asked.

Missy felt for a pulse and found the man's skin cold. "No, he's not okay," she turned white as a sheet. "He's dead."

Chapter 3

Detective Chas Beckett arrived at the scene via a rear entrance with several LaChance police officers in tow. They hadn't walked through the ballroom, not wanting to alarm the children as the party concluded. Missy had tried to call and text Ben several times, wanting to know where he was and if he was okay. It had been more than a bit traumatic finding a dead man in his costume. She and Loretta reviewed the course of events with the detective, trying to remember anything that could've been of significance. A forensics team had taken over the break room, gathering evidence that would hopefully not only shed some light on what had happened to Ben, but also help determine the identity of the dead man in the clown suit.

"Did either of you see anything that seemed out of the ordinary, or anyone who was behaving oddly?" Chas asked Missy and Loretta.

Both shook their heads. Missy had been wrapped up in keeping close watch over cupcake consumption, and Loretta had been working the room making sure that everyone was having a good time. The parents of the children in attendance had been in an adjacent, smaller ballroom, having cocktails and appetizers, and were notified that the party was ending sooner than anticipated, but were not given a reason why. Loretta discreetly circulated among the adult guests, looking for unfamiliar faces, but came up with nothing.

After all of the attendees had gone and the ballroom was deserted, Missy wandered aimlessly, worried sick about Ben, while Chas and his team examined every inch of the space. Loretta ushered out the remaining volunteers, pocketing Beckett's card in case she remembered anything that might be significant, and Missy reluctantly headed home, first eliciting a promise from Chas that he would come over when he was finished with the investigation.

On a hunch, Missy drove around the parking lot of the hotel looking for Ben's car, dismayed when she found it sitting in a space near the employee entrance. His car was there, but he was not. She peered in the windows of the little blue car, hoping to see some kind of clue, but found nothing that looked out of the ordinary. She texted Chas to tell him about the car, and received his assurance that he would check it out. Pulling out of the hotel parking lot, headed toward home, her phone rang. It was Cheryl, asking if Missy knew when Ben would be done. Missy gently told her what had happened, clenching her fist and biting the inside of her cheek to keep from crying, as the shocked girl sobbed into the phone. Promising that she would call the moment that she heard anything, Missy hung up after making sure that Cheryl was going to be okay. The girl was distraught, but regained control of her emotions, steadfastly refusing to believe that anything awful could have happened to a sweet, loving person like Ben.

Chapter 4

Missy's adoring golden retriever, Toffee, greeted her with her usual exuberance, when she opened the front door to her cozy, butter-yellow Victorian home, but the sensitive canine immediately picked up on her mistress's subdued mood. Toffee followed her from room to room as she put down her purse and keys, changed into walking clothes and gathered up the leash. Snapping the lead onto her furry companion's collar, Missy walked her to the park and back in a daze, worried sick about Ben. She knew that Chas would call her as soon as he was done at the hotel, but the waiting seemed endless.

Mechanically, Missy prepared dinner, despite her profound lack of appetite. At this point, she was on automatic pilot, falling back into routine because her thought process was numbed with worry. Focusing on menial tasks was much easier than letting her mind wander toward awful possibilities. Stirring a cup of gumbo around and around with her spoon, taking small tastes periodically as she stared into space, she waited for the phone to ring. Eventually, giving in and dumping the untasted portion back into her gumbo pot, she acknowledged that until she had some news, trying to eat was going to be nothing more than a waste of time and food.

Taking her phone with her, just in case, Missy ran a warm bath, hoping that it would calm her nerves and help her focus, and, although she knew that it was probably not a smart idea on an empty stomach, she poured a glass of mellow Merlot to sip while she bathed. Toffee curled up on a bath mat in the corner of the large bathroom, peering up at her best friend occasionally with concerned chocolate eyes. Finally, after exfoliating, moisturizing and dressing in a clean pair of yoga pants and a loose, comfy sweatshirt, Missy settled into the soft embrace of her overstuffed sofa, fully prepared to pretend to watch a movie, when the text tone on her phone pinged. Snatching it up from the arm of the couch, she saw that the message was from Chas, letting her know that he was on his way.

"So, what did you find out?" she demanded, dragging the handsome detective across the threshold and into the kitchen.

He seated himself in the breakfast nook and shook his head, looking frustrated. "Not much at all, unfortunately," he admitted grimly. "I looked at Ben's vehicle, and we procured a warrant to get it opened up, but found nothing of significance. There was a discarded cupcake wrapper beside the car that we're checking for prints and DNA, but, aside from that, our info is limited."

"What about the poor man in the clown suit? Did you find anything on him?" Missy asked, wide-eyed as she refilled her wine glass. "Would you like some?" she asked holding up her glass.

"No, thanks. I have a feeling that this isn't over yet this evening," Chas said, refusing the wine. "We don't have identification for the deceased yet, we'll be cross-checking his description with missing persons reports. I know that this is going to upset you, sweetie," he said, reaching for her hand, "but right now, with the significant lack of evidence that we've found, Ben is considered a person of interest in the murder."

"What?!" Missy exclaimed, horrified. "That boy is the kindest, sweetest soul that I know. There is no way in the world that he killed anyone. Do you even know how the man died?" she asked, taking her hand from his gentle grasp.

"Not yet, we'll have to wait for the autopsy results. If you hear anything from Ben, please let me know right away. I'm as reluctant as you are to believe that he had anything to do with the victim's death, but he'll need to be questioned properly, regardless," Beckett explained.

"Of course," she nodded. "Chas, honestly, I'm just hoping that whoever did this didn't hurt Ben too," she confessed, tears springing to her eyes.

"And I'd be lying if I told you that I didn't think that it's a possibility, but let's not make assumptions. I'm going to do everything that I can to find Ben, and hopefully he's safe and sound somewhere right now," the detective said, trying to be optimistic. He stroked the back of Missy's hand to reassure her, and his phone went off, startling them both. He glanced at the screen and picked up the call immediately. Missy could tell, by the brief questions that he asked, that he was speaking with someone regarding the case, but beyond that, the conversation wasn't enlightening her at all.

"Where?" Chas asked the caller. "When?" he said, looking at his watch. "Right. I'll be there in five minutes," he said, and tapped the End button on his phone.

"What is it? What's going on?" Missy asked, alarmed, as he stood quickly and headed for the front door.

"They found Ben, he's alive and waiting for questioning down at the station," Chas replied, his hand on the doorknob. "Stay here, and I'll let you know what happens," he directed in a tone meant to discourage further discussion.

"Absolutely not!" Missy insisted, sliding her feet into running shoes that were by the door and reaching for her coat. "I'm coming with you."

Beckett whirled to face her, trying to keep the frustration from his voice. "Look, sweetie, I know that you love Ben, and that you just want to help, but it would be entirely inappropriate to have you present during questioning. I'm conducting an investigation and as much as I'd like to include you, I have to play by the rules, okay?" he instructed. "I will keep you informed, and you know that I'll make sure we leave no stone unturned in trying to find the actual murderer, right?"

Missy nodded miserably. "Can you at least give him a hug for me?" she asked plaintively.

"No, I can't," Chas replied. "But I'll certainly let him know that you're thinking of him, when I have a moment."

"Thank you," she said, standing on tiptoe to kiss his cheek before he left.

"You're welcome," the handsome detective kissed her back. "Try to get some sleep, I have a feeling that it's going to be a long night."

Chapter 5

Missy's jaw dropped in shock when Ben showed up at Missy's Frosted Love Cupcakes the next morning, ready to put in a full work day, as though nothing had happened.

"Ben, what are you doing here?" she exclaimed, wrapping him in a bear hug.

"Stocking the cases for opening," he replied mildly.

Missy pulled back, holding him at arm's length, examining his face to see if he looked any worse for the wear after what could've only been a tremendous ordeal for him. "Are you okay? Tell me what happened," she asked, frowning with concern.

"Umm…I will, but…" he began, hesitant.

"But what? What is it?" his boss interrupted.

"Well, it's just that, we have this huge line out front and we need to get these people their cupcakes," he explained, gesturing to the front of the store.

Missy stared at him with surprise and admiration. "Yes, we do, don't we?" she grinned. "Let's get these folks taken care of, and then you're going to sit down with me over coffee and cupcakes and tell me all about it."

"Yes ma'am," Ben said agreeably, heading for the front door to flip over the Open sign.

Missy's curiosity clawed at her unbearably as she, Chris and Ben weathered the first massive wave of morning customers, and it seemed like an eternity until the line died down enough that they could finally entrust Chris with the running the front counter on his own. Grabbing a couple of the Cupcakes of the Day, she instructed Ben to pour two cups of coffee before joining her in the employee break room.

"Mmm...what are these?" Ben asked through a giant mouthful of cupcake.

"My new Orange Dream recipe. I used orange juice in the batter, filled them with vanilla cream cheese, and infused the icing with orange zest," she answered impatiently. "Now, tell me what happened at the party, and at the police station last night," she demanded.

Still marveling over the cupcake, which tasted just like the orange and vanilla popsicles that he used to buy from the ice cream truck as a kid, Ben took a sip of coffee to wash down the huge bite before responding.

"I had taken the big papier-mâché clown head off and put it on the table in the break room so that I could eat my cupcake and have some of the punch that I snagged before I left, and the next thing I knew, someone really strong had clamped an oddly sweet-smelling cloth over my mouth, and I passed out or something."

"Oh, my goodness, Ben, that's awful! Did you see who did that to you?" Missy asked, on the edge of her seat.

Swallowing another bite of Orange Dream, the LaChance manager shook his head slowly. "I have no idea. It all happened so fast. He came out of nowhere."

Missy frowned, thinking. "So, this happened right when you sat down? You didn't have a chance to eat your cupcake?" she demanded.

"Nope, as far as I know, it's still sitting on the table in the break room," he shrugged. "Why?"

"Because Chas…er, Detective Beckett said that they found the empty cupcake paper dropped beside your car. So, if you didn't eat it, maybe the killer did," she deduced. "And if that's the case, hopefully they'll get some idea as to his identity from it."

"Wait…" Ben seemed suddenly alarmed. "Killer? What are you talking about?"

Missy raised her eyebrows in surprise. "They didn't tell you? Oh, my goodness," she muttered, wondering if she had done something wrong by letting the cat out of the bag with Ben. Well, there was no hiding it now. "They found an unidentified man in the break room after you went missing. He was dead and wearing your clown costume."

"That's why they told me that they were holding the costume for evidence," the young man mused. "Wait…they don't think that I did it, do they?" he asked, horrified at the thought.

Missy's face answered his question, and his shoulders sagged. "Where were you, Ben? What happened to you after you were drugged?"

He shrugged miserably. "I have no idea. All I know is that I woke up laying under a bush in a park in Smithville."

"Smithville? That's at least 40 miles from here! How did you end up there? And why?" she wondered, puzzled.

"That's what I was wondering. I was still a little woozy from whatever was used to make me pass out, but I knew that something weird was going on, so I called 911 and the police came and picked me up. They dropped me off at the police station in LaChance and I spent the next few hours answering a bunch of questions that made no sense," he recounted. "Makes sense now," he sighed. "You know I could never hurt anyone, don't you, Ms. G.?"

"Of course I know that, Ben," she reassured the rattled young man. "But we need to think about who would've done this, and why. Do you have anyone who might be mad at you?"

"Not that I know of," he shook his head. "I do well in my classes, but not so well that I wreck the curve. Maybe some guy who has a crush on Cheryl found out that I proposed and freaked out?" he guessed, grasping at straws.

"Maybe," Missy frowned. She leaned forward, placing a comforting hand on his arm. "Whatever happened, Ben, Chas will figure it out. The best thing that you can do is to just keep living your life one day at a time until the truth comes out."

He nodded slowly, the reality of his situation hitting hard. "Do you mind if Chris closes up without me today?" he asked quietly. "I really just want to go talk to Cheryl and let her know what's going on."

"Of course, honey," Missy agreed without hesitation. "She

should be done closing up the Dellville shop by the time you drive over. Go ahead and go, Chris and I can manage closing here," she stood.

"Thanks," he said, head down, giving her a quick hug on his way out.

Missy sadly watched him go, knowing exactly what it felt like to be mistakenly accused. She silently vowed to do whatever it took to exonerate the conscientious young man.

Chapter 6

"Any breaks?" Missy asked Detective Chas Beckett across the red and white oilcloth-covered table at their favorite crawfish restaurant.

"Not really," Chas sighed, digging his fork into the heaping pile of Shrimp Étouffée on his plate.

Missy pulled a corner off of the most dense, moist cornbread in the parish and popped it into her mouth. "I'm worried about Ben," she confessed. "There are dark circles under his eyes that make me think that he hasn't been sleeping, and I'd swear that he's lost weight, poor boy," she frowned.

"Well, as of right now, he's the only person of interest in the case, unfortunately. We haven't been able to identify the deceased yet, and the DNA from the cupcake wrapper is still at the lab, along with fiber evidence collected from the costume. We did have one of the cocktail servers from the adult party say that he seemed to recall a man in a tuxedo coming out of the break room just before the body was discovered, but the description that he gave was so vague that it could've been anyone," Chas drained his glass of tea and their aging waitress came over with a refill, temporarily stalling the conversation.

"Chas, Ben didn't do this," Missy asserted after the waitress moved on.

"I believe that, I really do," he assured her. "I'm working as hard as I can to figure out who did it, so that Ben can go on with his life."

Missy went to the Dellville shop after lunch to help Grayson, Cheryl's pale skinned, dark-haired young assistant, pack up an order for a church social. When she came in the back entrance to the commercial kitchen, the sensitive youth pulled her immediately aside, his dark eyes wide.

"Ms. G.," he said quietly, looking around as though making certain that he wasn't being overheard. "I'm really worried about Cheryl. She has hardly said a word all day, and she keeps running back to the break room. One time, I stood outside the door and heard her crying. I don't know what's going on, but something is clearly wrong."

"Okay, darlin, thanks for the heads up. Is it slow enough that you'll be able to handle the front alone while I talk to her?" Missy asked.

Grayson nodded vehemently. "Yes, ma'am, whatever it takes. I'll be fine. I just hope that Cheryl is okay."

"I'm sure she will be. Why don't you go up front and send her back to talk to me, okay?" Missy directed.

"I will," the youth assured her, disappearing through the entrance to the front of the shop, where Cheryl was restocking the cases.

Her sweet-natured and efficient manager appeared a few seconds after Grayson's departure. "You wanted to see me, Ms. G.?"

"Cheryl, honey, what's wrong?" Missy asked, foregoing meaningless greetings and pretense.

The young woman's face crumpled into tears at Missy's question, and she put her hands over her eyes, her defenses breaking down entirely. Heartbroken at the sight of her suffering, Missy went to her, embracing the trembling girl.

"Oh honey, what is it? You can tell me. I guarantee that whatever it is, you'll feel better after talking about it," she smoothed Cheryl's hair, holding her while she cried. When her sobs turned to sniffles, Missy held her at arm's length, forcing her to look at her and commanded gently, "Tell me."

"Ben…" she began, her lower lip trembling and tears threatening anew.

"What about Ben?" Missy prompted gently.

"He…he broke off our engagement," she dissolved into tears again.

"What?" Missy exclaimed, astonished. "Why would he do such a thing?"

"He said that he didn't want me to have to go through life with someone who had been accused of murder," Cheryl cried, distraught. "I know he didn't do it, Ms. G., I don't care what anyone says, but he said that small towns can be cruel when it comes to such things and he didn't want me to have to go through that."

"Well, I'm sure he's just upset. You and I both know that he loves you very much, he's just not thinking clearly at the moment, which is completely understandable after the ordeal that he went through," she soothed. "Listen to me, sugar, you are the most important thing in that young man's life. He needs you and he knows it, he's just confused right now because he's in a very scary situation. Give him some time, but don't give up. He'll come to his senses soon enough, okay?" Missy took a tissue out of the purse that she had set down on the counter and handed it to the sniffling young woman.

"It just really hurts to have him push me away, just when he needs me most," Cheryl confessed miserably.

"I know, honey," Missy squeezed her arm supportively. "But right now, you're going to have to be the strong one. Just be there for him. He'll figure it out in his own time," she hugged her again.

"I know, he's a good man. I couldn't ask for anyone better. Ms. G., would it be okay if I went home a little early today? I'm not feeling very well."

"Of course, sugar. You head on home, I'll stay here and make sure that Grayson has backup if he needs it, don't you worry. Have a bite to eat, get some rest, and things will look better in the morning," she advised. "You call me if you need me, okay?"

"Yes ma'am, thanks," Cheryl failed miserably in her attempt to smile.

Chapter 7

Missy's heart was heavy as she drove home after helping Grayson close up her Dellville shop. Cheryl and Ben were two amazing human beings whose lives had been turned upside down, and she felt helpless to do anything about it. She also felt quite a bit of guilt, knowing that the only reason that Ben had been at the party in the first place was because she had called him to come in and save the day. So, in the process of lending a helping hand in order to make children smile and raise money for a local charity, the unfortunate young man had become a murder suspect.

Frustrated, Missy pulled into her driveway, ready to go for a nice long run with Toffee to work off some of her anxiety. She typically pulled into the garage and entered the house from the back porch, but as she drove past the front of her home, she noticed what looked like a manila envelope stuck between the heavy mahogany front door and surrounding frame, so she left her little burgundy car in the driveway, and trotted up the porch steps to retrieve the parcel.

Her name and address were on the front of the envelope,

which had apparently been dropped off by someone from the offices of Parker, LeBlanc and Christianson, Attorneys at Law. Thinking that the correspondence was likely from Loretta Christianson, perhaps thanking her for her donation and time, she tossed it on the kitchen table, heading upstairs to change for some serious time in the park with her prancing and frolicking retriever. A comically rigorous game of fetch with Toffee was just the medicine that Missy needed to shake off her worry and sadness, even if just for a while, to regain some sense of perspective. By the time the daring duo headed home from the park, both were happily worn out. The text tone on Missy's phone pinged, shortly after they got in the door, alerting her to a text from Chas. The dashing detective had texted to request the pleasure of her company at his house for dinner and a movie, which after the day she'd had, sounded just heavenly.

After taking care of Toffee's dinner and filling a bowl with fresh, cool water for the panting animal, Missy jogged up the stairs to shower and dress for dinner. She selected an outfit of jeans and a sumptuous blue angora sweater that was entirely appropriate for winter in Louisiana, pulled her blonde curls up into a messy bun, and highlighted her soft grey eyes with just a touch of eyeliner and mascara. It may only be an "at-home date," but she wanted to look casually pretty when the tall-dark-and-handsome detective opened his door.

An evening with Chas was just what she needed. Good wine, good food and good company sounded like the perfect combination to help her relax, and the detective's calming presence nearly always served to restore her optimism.

"Hey, beautiful," he greeted her with a smile when she opened his front door and found him in the kitchen. She nestled into his embrace, resting her cheek on the hard planes of his muscular chest, and took comfort in the simple, regular sound of his heartbeat, as Toffee made herself at home on the dog bed that he kept for her in the living room.

"I'm so glad to see you," she murmured, content within the circle of his arms.

"You okay?" he asked, stepping back a bit so that he could look into her eyes, and relieved when there were no tears.

"Yeah, I'm good," Missy nodded. "I'm worried about Ben of course, but I'm determined to enjoy myself tonight anyway."

"Yeah…about that…" Chas began, looking concerned.

"Oh no…what? Did you find something?" she interrupted.

"Let's have some dinner and we'll discuss it," the detective placed his hand on the small of her back, gently directing her toward the dining room, where the table was set casually with everyday plates and utensils, a bottle of Italian red wine, and two boxes from Missy's favorite pizzeria. He'd used red linen napkins, and red tapers to solidify the theme, and while Missy was delighted at his thoughtfulness, she was too curious about what was happening with the investigation to pay much attention to her surroundings.

Chas pulled out her chair for her, then took the seat directly across the table, reaching for her plate and placed two large slices of combination pizza on it. The melted cheese stretched between the slices as he pulled them out of the box in a way that normally would have made Missy's mouth water, but at the moment, she was preoccupied with thoughts of Ben.

"So, what's going on?" she asked, biting the tip off of her slice of pizza.

"We've identified the body," the detective said, shaking extra parmesan on top of his heaping plate.

"Well, that's good news, isn't it?" she interrupted again, impatient to hear something positive.

"Typically, yes, because most crimes aren't random. Victims generally know their killers, and the association that they have can lead right to the perpetrator," he explained, holding something back.

"Wait…" Missy frowned. "You said, 'typically' identifying the victim is a positive thing. Why wouldn't it be in this case?" she asked, dreading the answer.

"The victim was Stanley Conner," Chas replied, as though that explained it all. When his pronouncement was greeted with nothing more than a blank look, he continued, "Cheryl's stepfather."

Missy was confused. "That's strange, I thought that Cheryl didn't have any family around here."

"She doesn't. Conner is from out of state. We did a little digging and discovered that he left town a few years ago, after Cheryl's mom died under very suspicious circumstances. It was before I came to LaChance, but guys who were on the force at the time said that, even though it looked like Stanley Conner had killed his wife, Cheryl's mom, the DA felt like there wasn't enough evidence to convict, so he was never brought to trial," he explained.

Missy's mouth fell open in surprise. "Well, that would certainly explain why the poor girl never mentioned having a stepfather. I had no idea that her mother was murdered, how terribly sad."

Chas nodded, avoiding her gaze.

"What?" Missy asked suspiciously, realizing that he wasn't telling her the whole story.

He gave her a pained look and answered reluctantly. "The unfortunate thing in all of this is that, determining the identity of the victim only served to strengthen the idea that Ben might be the perpetrator, and if he's not…the scrutiny will most likely fall upon Cheryl."

"That's utterly ridiculous," Missy exclaimed, pushing her plate away. "Cheryl is entirely incapable of harming anyone."

"Her statement given after her mother's death would seem to indicate otherwise," Beckett said gently.

"What do you mean?" she narrowed her eyes, not wanting to believe that the sweet girl who had worked diligently for her was capable of a heinous crime.

"She made no secret of the fact that she thought that Stanley had killed her mother, and made several statements regarding her desire to see him imprisoned for life."

"Which is completely understandable under the circumstances," Missy shot back, defending the girl.

"Yes, it is," Chas agreed. "But it also implies some pretty intense feelings of hostility toward a murder victim who just happened to be found dead inside her boyfriend's clown costume."

"But how would Cheryl have even known that Stanley was in town? And I'm almost positive that Ben couldn't have known who he was. He never mentioned anything to me, and wasn't acting strangely at all. He wouldn't have even been at the event if I hadn't called him. Which I really wish I hadn't after everything that's happened," she sighed, shaking her head. "Why was Stanley Conner even in LaChance to begin with?"

"We don't know, but he was a nurse at the hospital when he lived here, so it's plausible that he heard about the event and wanted to attend," the detective mused.

"Was he on the guest list?"

"No. That's the wrench in the works. He wasn't invited, and yet he was there. I'm hoping that when we find out the reason for his return to LaChance, it'll lead us to the murderer."

Missy's eyes widened. "Oh no…" she whispered, feeling slightly ill.

"What?" Beckett asked, leaning forward and taking her hand.

Missy raised her eyes to meet his and replied woodenly, "What if Stanley was in town because he heard that Cheryl was engaged?"

"That would mean that he'd potentially been in contact with her, and she could have known that he would be attending the event," Chas admitted ruefully.

"Oh, my goodness, Chas…do you think she could have possibly…?" Missy couldn't bring herself to even finish the sentence, staring at the detective wide-eyed and clutching his hand.

"She could have," he nodded. "Or, perhaps even worse…she could have prompted her fiancé to do it for her, or with her," Chas gazed at Missy gravely.

Missy shook her head vehemently in disbelief. "No. I can't believe that. I won't. Not about Ben. I know he loves her, but

I refuse to believe that he would do such a thing," her mouth in a stubborn line.

"Cheryl's coming in for questioning tomorrow morning. She doesn't know the identity of the victim, and I need you to promise me that you won't tell her. I have a feeling that once we speak to her, we'll have a better idea as to how we need to proceed with the investigation," he said quietly, brushing away a tear that had rolled down Missy's cheek. "Let's not jump to any conclusions just yet. We don't have all of the lab results back, and it's usually the evidence that tells the tale."

Missy was so worn out and defeated after speaking with Chas about the case, that she elected to skip the movie to go home and take a bubble bath before bed. She spotted the manila envelope from Parker, LeBlanc and Christianson that she had entirely forgotten, and picked it up on her way upstairs, figuring that it would be nice to read a pleasant thank you from Loretta after all the potentially bad news that she'd just received. Bending back the small brass wings that held the envelope shut, she reached in, expecting a sweet, handmade card, and pulled out a multi-paged legal document. Too tired to make heads or tails of it at the moment, she stuffed it back in the envelope, knowing that Chas would help her interpret the legalese in the morning.

Chapter 8

"According to this, a Dr. Bernard Radcliffe Aston is alleging that a representative of your company, namely, Ben, gave his vegan, celiac daughter a normal cupcake during the children's party at the hotel, which resulted in a reaction so severe that it necessitated a hospital stay," Chas said, scanning the stack of legal documents. "He's suing Ben, you as a person, and you as a business owner, for the cost of the hospital stay and damages. He's also alleging that you are a danger to the community, and is asking for punitive damages which include both of your stores being closed down. With the language in this suit, it's looks like there could be criminal implications as well as civil ones, if he elects to press charges," Chas gave Missy the bad news, after reading over the documents from the manila envelope.

The color drained from Missy's face and she swayed on her feet.

"That's ridiculous," she murmured, heartsick. "We'd never hurt anyone, much less a child. Ben had nothing to do with the cupcakes. He didn't give any out, he was too busy making balloon animals and singing funny songs. If anyone is to blame, it's me, but I'm certain that I didn't give any regular cupcakes out to a child with warning wristbands on," she frowned, certain that she was right. Missy thought for a moment, then glanced up at the detective in utter terror. "Chas...I could lose...everything," she whispered, tears of fear and frustration welling in her eyes.

"Not to mention the fact that this lawsuit is going to cast an even more negative light upon Ben, as well," the detective pointed out. "First, he's suspected of murder, and now, he may be held accountable for physical damage done to a child," Chas recounted the grim reality.

"What are we going to do?" Missy worried, at a loss.

"It's time to talk with an attorney."

Missy dialed Loretta Christianson's number, thinking that, because her husband was an attorney, she'd surely know who to call for someone in her situation.

"Loretta speaking," the organizer sang out upon answering her phone.

"Hi, Loretta, it's Missy Gladstone. I hate to bother you but..." Missy began, only to be rudely cut off.

"I have nothing to say to you, Melissa. I trusted you with the health and well-being of innocent young children, and your incompetence endangered one of those precious young lives. I'm glad my husband is the one suing you, you should be ashamed of yourself," she accused, hanging up before Missy could even get a word in edgewise.

When she heard the click of Loretta's phone disconnecting, Missy looked at her phone in dismay. Not only was she being unfairly accused, but in a town the size of LaChance, having an enemy as powerful as Loretta Christianson could be financially devastating as well as socially uncomfortable. Stomach churning with fear and shame, Missy laid her head down on her kitchen table and cried. Dear, gentle Toffee came over and put her head on Missy's knee, entirely unsurprised when her best friend slid down to the floor and buried a tear-stained face into her coat.

Chapter 9

Missy had been avoiding Cheryl because she didn't know what to say to her. She couldn't shake the thought that the sweet-seeming girl may very well have killed her stepfather, but when she received a text from her that said "*911, please call me at the shop,*" she knew she had no choice but to respond.

"Hi Cheryl, it's Missy. What's going on?"

The young woman sounded panicked and spoke in a low voice. "Is there any way that you can come into the shop? I've had people calling me all morning to cancel their delivery and party orders. I have no idea what's going on, and none of them will tell me why they're cancelling. I don't know what's happening, or what to do."

Missy sighed, guessing that Loretta Christianson had been on the warpath, convincing the many friends that she had in various businesses, churches and organizations that Missy's cupcakes were not to be trusted. "Okay, Cheryl, I'll be over there in a few, just make a stack of the requests to cancel, and

I'll call them back to see what I can find out," she directed, picking up her keys to head to the Dellville shop. She knew that Chris and Ben would be more than able to handle the trickle of customers who might happen to wander into the LaChance location.

Missy was numb. The LaChance shop had been started by her parents, decades ago, and passed on to her after their tragic deaths when she was just seventeen. Baking for a living was the only life she'd ever known, and the thought of her beloved shops closing filled her with an unspeakable dread. She had to fight the lawsuit. One way or another, the truth had to set her free. She couldn't fathom any other option.

Going directly to her office, Missy did her best to avoid Cheryl, her greeting to the bewildered girl polite but short. Grayson and Cheryl exchanged a puzzled look at the owner's cool indifference, but shrugged it off and kept working. Most of the patrons who had cancelled didn't answer Missy's calls, but the ones who did gave vague excuses and got off the phone as soon as possible. Some of them seemed quite cold to her, and after dealing with so many people who were just shy of being rude, she leaned her head in her hand and dumped the rest of the cancellation requests in the trash.

Feeling as though her world was falling apart, she gathered her purse and stood to leave. A soft knock on her doorframe caused her to turn.

"Ms. G., is everything okay?" Cheryl asked quietly, concern written all over her face.

"No, actually, nothing is okay, but I'm dealing with it the best way that I know how," Missy snapped, immediately ashamed of her tone.

"It's about me, isn't it? It's because they think that I killed Stanley," she mumbled, embarrassed. "You don't think that I did it, do you?" she asked pitifully.

Missy eyed her sadly for a long moment before responding.

"I have no idea what to think," she said tiredly, brushing past the miserable girl. "You can let Grayson close up by himself if you need to go home. I don't think we're going to be getting much business for a while," she tossed over her shoulder, heading out the door.

When Ben called a few minutes later, asking if Chris could close up the LaChance store so that he could drive over and give Cheryl a ride home, she felt a twinge of conscience, knowing that the poor girl had probably fallen apart after she left. Taking the guilt over her treatment of Cheryl out on Ben, she told him that he needed to make sure that everything at the LaChance store was taken care of before he picked up his distraught former fiancé, knowing full well that he would never consider leaving his work undone. He sounded hurt when he hung up, making Missy feel like a first-class heel, but she allowed her frustration to convince her that she didn't care, she was just being the boss.

Driving home, Missy felt her fear and frustration building within her to the point where she felt like she just might explode. Charging up the back porch steps, she ran up to her bedroom and changed into exercise wear. Toffee, who had been at her heels from the moment that she came in, wagged her tail excitedly when Missy jogged back downstairs and snapped the leash onto her collar. Taking the usual backpack of items, dog and owner headed to the park. Missy could walk, run and toss her frustrations about, and Toffee would joyfully be on the receiving end of it. The two ran and played hard for over an hour, then headed home for dinner.

After a long, hot shower, Missy made a simple meal of red beans and rice with slices of spicy andouille, and curled up on the couch to find escape in a movie. The text tone on her phone pinged and she picked it up, seeing a message from Chas.

"There's been an accident. I'm five minutes away from your house and will pick you up."

Missy couldn't imagine what kind of accident Chas might be talking about, but accidents in general were never good, so her heart rate accelerated a bit as she reached for her shoes. She ran a quick brush through her hair, and heard Toffee enthusiastically greeting the handsome detective. She practically flew down the stairs.

"What accident? What happened?" she asked breathlessly.

"Ben lost control of his car and it went over an embankment. He and Cheryl are in the hospital. She's conscious, but is pretty shaken up, and Ben..." he hesitated.

"Ben what? What about Ben?" Missy panicked, grabbing Beckett's arm.

"He has a head injury and hasn't regained consciousness yet," the detective broke the news to her as gently as possible.

Her hands went to her throat as tears welled. "Oh, my goodness, Chas, is he going to be okay?" she whispered.

"I don't know, sweetie. I wish I did," he pulled her into a brief embrace, then led her out the door.

Cheryl was being questioned by a police officer when they

arrived, and would be allowed to go home with bandages and pain meds as soon as they were finished. Ben was in intensive care, and couldn't have any visitors as yet, so Missy and Chas sat in the IC waiting room, hoping for the best. The officer who had been speaking with Cheryl when they came in, entered the waiting room quietly and asked to speak with Chas, who left the room with him immediately.

Missy shivered in the chilly waiting room. The chairs were uncomfortably firm and covered in a waterproof, stain-proof fabric which featured a pattern of green leaves on a dark purple background. A vending machine hummed in the corner, and the scent of hand-sanitizer and antiseptics permeated the space. Missy noticed that it was the most cold, impersonal room that she had been in in quite some time, and felt somehow that she deserved to be in the imposing space. She berated herself for being nasty and short with both Ben and Cheryl before their accident.

She didn't know what she'd do if something awful happened to Ben. He just had to get well, so that she could apologize to him and thank him for his loyalty and hard work. He was like family to her and she'd mistreated him because she was worried and stressed. Cheryl was a new addition, but family nonetheless, and she had treated her poorly because she may have committed a crime of passion. Missy didn't know whether the girl was innocent or guilty, but, if she was being honest, she hadn't even given her the benefit of doubt.

She stood when Chas came back in, looking at him expectantly. He sat down next to her to explain what he had found out from the investigating officer.

"Cheryl said that they were driving along just fine, but when they came to the part of Sheldon Road that has a steep incline with a curve at the bottom, Ben tried to use the brakes and they didn't work, so the car slid right through the guard rail and over the embankment. The ground was muddy and soft because of the rain we've had recently, which cushioned the fall a bit, but the car didn't stop moving until it hit a tree, which smashed in Ben's door and gave him the head injury. The rescue crew had to cut the top of the car off to get him to safety."

Missy had begun crying as Chas described the series of events, and shook her head in horror as he finished. "Oh Chas, that's awful," she cried. "But it's so strange that Ben's brakes didn't work. He's meticulous about maintaining his car."

"That's one of the disturbing details," the detective grimaced. "After Cheryl told the officer who was interviewing her about the brakes, he had another guy on the scene check out the car, and they discovered that the brake lines had been punctured."

Missy's hands flew to her mouth in horror. "You mean some-one…" she couldn't finish the sentence.

Chas nodded. "Someone either wanted Ben hurt, or…"

"Dead," Missy whispered. "But who would do such a thing? Ben is a sweet, innocent young man."

"Maybe someone who didn't want him to confess what he knows about the murder," the detective raised his eyebrows.

"Cheryl?" Missy whispered, utterly horrified.

Beckett opened his mouth to answer, closing it again when a doctor walked into the room.

"Detective Beckett?" the doctor asked, ignoring Missy entirely.

"Yes, and you are?" Chas asked holding out his hand.

The doctor shook it perfunctorily. "Dr. Aston," was the terse response. "I've been monitoring Ben Radigan's progress. He seems to have stabilized, but has not yet regained consciousness. Since I'm assuming that you have better things to do, I'll advise you that sitting here, waiting, is really just a waste of time. We'll notify your office when…or if, he regains consciousness," he said, without the slightest touch of compassion.

Missy stood, wanting to speak to him before he left the room. "Dr. Aston, my name is Meliss…" she began before he cut her off.

"I know who you are, and I have nothing to say to you," he said, arrogantly. "Detective," he nodded in Chas's direction, and left the room.

"Chas!" Missy grabbed the detective's arm. "Isn't this some sort of conflict of interest? I don't feel comfortable with the fact that Ben's doctor is the man who is suing us," her voice was insistent. "You saw how uncaring he seemed. What if he tries to get back at Ben by not giving him proper care?" her fingers dug into Chas's well-sculpted bicep.

The detective placed a comforting arm around her shoulders, leading her from the room. "Let's maintain a little bit of perspective here, shall we? There's no way that Dr. Bernard Aston would throw away his career just because he was angry and involved in a lawsuit. His responsibilities as a caregiver are the same, regardless of whom he's treating," he explained gently. "I know you're upset, but we just have to trust that

Ben is in good hands. He's a young, strong guy – he'll be fine," he assured her.

Missy wrapped her arms around her midsection, miserable and sick with fear for Ben.

"Would you feel better bringing Toffee over and staying at my place tonight?" Chas asked, at a loss as to how to comfort her.

Missy shook her head and avoided his concerned gaze, knowing that just the look in his eyes might cause the dam of her emotions to burst.

"No, I'll be fine at home. I'm just going to go to bed," she replied numbly.

Chapter 10

Missy lay under her hand-stitched quilt, staring into the darkness of her room. Sleep seemed an impossibility as her mind whirled with thoughts, doubts, fears and anger. In the morning, she would have to close her Dellville store, because Cheryl would need to stay home and recover from the accident, and even with the decrease in traffic, she couldn't expect Grayson to run it by himself all day every day. She had called to let the sensitive youth know that he needed to report to the LaChance store the next day. He agreed immediately, wanting to do whatever he could to help. Little did Missy know that, since he didn't have a car, he'd have to get up extra early and ride his bike to LaChance, thanking his lucky stars that at least Louisiana winters were generally pretty mild. Had she known, Missy would've picked him up herself, but the polite young man didn't want to impose, so he kept his transportation woes to himself.

Both of her managers were unable to work, leaving one shop closed entirely, and the other staffed by two assistants and herself. Determined to have a business for Ben to return to, she planned to rise to the occasion and bravely tough out her circumstances as best she could. A small cluster of customers had remained faithful to the LaChance store, despite Loretta Christianson's gossip. Missy was more than aware that if Cheryl was arrested for murder, she'd have to hire someone else to fill the position in Dellville, and that probability seemed more and more likely, but her staffing issues were among the least important things on her mind at the moment.

When the blessed oblivion of sleep finally claimed her, she was tormented by dreams that left her feeling weary and unrefreshed. It was with great effort, and more than a measure of reluctance that Missy peeled her eyes open in the morning, knowing that she had to face the day, whether she was ready for it or not. Her first order of business, after letting Toffee out, was a phone call to Chas to check on Ben's progress. The young manager had been moved out of the ICU and into his own room, but had not yet regained consciousness. She made plans to visit him after breakfast, and headed over to the LaChance store to see how Grayson and Chris were doing.

Pleased that things were operating smoothly, even without the guidance and supervision of management, Missy felt comfortable leaving the guys at the LaChance store so that she could drop in and visit Ben. Arriving at his room with a teddy bear, an elaborate arrangement of flowers and a bouquet of helium mylar "Get Well" balloons, she was surprised to see Cheryl, bruised and bandaged, sitting miserably in a mauve faux leather recliner in a corner of Ben's room.

"Hi, Ms. G.," the young woman greeted her tentatively, as

Missy placed her colorful gifts on the window sill where Ben would see them when he woke up.

"Hi, Cheryl. How are you feeling?" Missy asked quietly, fussing with the flowers, barely able to look at her.

"Everything hurts," she admitted with a slight shrug. "But, all things considered, I was the lucky one," her faced was pained as she gazed at her comatose former fiancé.

"No progress?" Missy gazed at Ben, her heart breaking.

Cheryl shook her head, tears welling in her eyes. "What am I going to do if he never…" her voice choked off as she struggled not to cry.

"We can't think in those terms," Missy asserted, having had the same thought process the night before. "We're not going to give up on him. He's strong, he'll get through this," she said, with more conviction than she felt. "How long have you been here?"

"Visiting hours are from 8 a.m. to 8 p.m., so I've been here since 7:30. I waited in the coffeeshop downstairs until it was time to come up," she said, staring at the floor. She sighed and raised her eyes to meet Missy's, looking as though she was drowning in despair. "Please don't hate me, Ms. G. I swear to you, I didn't hurt anyone. I don't know who killed my stepfather, or why, but it wasn't me," her eyes begged for understanding that Missy wasn't quite prepared to give.

"Let's just concentrate on you and Ben getting better, okay?" she said, pitying the pale young woman before her, but not quite trusting her.

Cheryl nodded sadly, returning her gaze to the floor, and tucked her feet up under her in the chair, her arms crossed over her chest, as though a chill that couldn't be eliminated gripped her. Missy moved to the side of Ben's bed, taking in all the tubes and wires attached to the young man whom she loved like a son. She swallowed a lump in her throat and patted his hand.

"Take all the time you need, but come back to us, sugar. We're waiting for you," she whispered.

Chapter 11

Missy's daily routine now consisted of a disturbing rhythm which included, checking on Grayson and Chris every morning, and delivering any orders that had been placed through the LaChance store, followed by a visit to Ben's room, haunted by the shadow of a girl perched in the corner chair, then back home to interrogate her boyfriend about the case and run out her anxieties with Toffee. She wasn't sleeping well, and had no interest in food, even leaving the baking of cupcakes for the shop to Grayson, who had an incredible aptitude for it. Despite her lack of appetite, she agreed to meet Chas for lunch at the local steakhouse.

"I just don't understand it, Chas," Missy complained, cutting tiny bits from her perfectly-cooked ribeye. "Ben is still not waking up. I'm sorry, I know you feel that we should trust Dr. Aston, but I just don't. He didn't act like any doctor that I've ever seen. Even if we're in the midst of legal action, he could've at least spoken compassionately about Ben."

"I've run into some top-notch doctors whose bedside manners are horrible. When Aston spoke with me, it was from one professional to another, he has no idea that Ben means anything to me, so he didn't feel the need for diplomacy or tact, he just presented the facts," Chas shrugged. "I'm sure Ben is getting the best care possible."

"Well, I'm not so sure. Dr. Aston was positively nasty to me, and I can't help but think that if he's so bitter about what happened to his daughter, he might just take it out on Ben. Isn't there some way that you can check up on his success record? Maybe see if he's made poor decisions in the past, which negatively impacted any of his patients? It'd make me feel so much better if I believed that he was actually a good doctor, even if he's a cold human being."

"Sure, if it'll make you feel better, I'll do some checking," he assured her, adding a dash of salt to his fluffy baked potato. "In the meantime, please just try to relax, okay?"

Missy nodded and speared a green bean with her fork, nibbling the end of it. A man walking in with a thin, beautiful blonde woman caught her eye, and she realized that it was none other than Sidney Christianson, Loretta's husband and the lawyer who was suing her on Dr. Aston's behalf.

"Don't be obvious about it, but when you have a moment, take a look at the table in the corner. The man sitting there is Sidney Christianson, but I don't recognize the woman," she leaned forward and whispered, pretending to be reaching for the salt.

Chas nodded, chewing a bite of steak. After he swallowed and washed down the bite with a sip of sweet tea, he casually glanced to his left and took in the occupants of the corner table. "Interesting," he remarked, turning back to Missy.

"What? What's interesting?" her curiosity was piqued.

"Well, I could be wrong, but if my memory of the society pages is correct, I believe that Christianson is with Mrs. Aston," he said in a low voice.

"As in Dr. Aston's wife?" Missy asked, eyebrows raised. When Chas nodded, she looked over again, subtly using her peripherals. "Looks to me like they have a bit cozier relationship than just that of lawyer and client," she whispered, observing the way that the couple was interacting.

"That was my thought too," Chas agreed. "Like I said, interesting."

Not wanting to be seen by the lawyer who was threatening to destroy her life as she knew it, Missy slipped out of the restaurant via a rear door near the restrooms, while Chas had their lunch boxed up and paid the check.

* * *

Despite the odd sighting of Sidney Christianson with Mrs. Aston, Missy, strangely, felt a bit better after lunch, confident that Chas would find something suspicious when he looked into Dr. Aston's history, and perhaps that of his wandering wife. She went back to check on Ben and once more found Cheryl sitting, waiting, in the corner.

"Do you stay here all day?" she asked the tortured young woman in the shadows.

Cheryl nodded, responding quietly. "They're pretty strict about visiting hours, but I stay as long as I'm allowed."

"What about meals?" Missy frowned, noticing that the young woman's clothes were baggy, and her cheeks seemed sunken beneath the bruises and scrapes.

"I'm not hungry. Sometimes I eat when I go home, other times I just can't make myself do it," she hugged her knees to her chest.

"I could make you some cupcakes," Missy offered, concerned. "Which kind are your favorites?" She might suspect the girl of murder, but she could not stand idly by while the pitiful creature starved to death.

"Please don't go to the trouble, I wouldn't be able to eat them anyway," Cheryl admitted. "Food doesn't taste good, and I stopped feeling hungry a few days ago."

"That's not healthy," her boss warned, heart torn between mistrust and compassion.

"I'm healthier than he is," she replied, her eyes glued on Ben. "This shouldn't have happened to him. It should have been me. I'd give anything to trade places with him," she murmured, seemingly forgetting that Missy present, rocking slightly back and forth. Missy moved to the bed, and after kissing Ben's forehead, slipped quietly from the room. Cheryl either didn't notice or simply didn't acknowledge her leaving.

Chapter 12

Curious about the relationship between Sidney Christianson and the coolly beautiful Mrs. Aston, Missy decided to do a bit of her own detective work. Her search for truth would most likely end up having absolutely nothing to do with her lawsuit, or the possible charges facing Ben and/or Cheryl, but it would at least give her something to do besides sitting around waiting for the results of the police investigation. After spending a little over an hour on her computer, Missy was able to track down the address of Dr. and Mrs. Aston, and decided to go for a drive that just happened to take her past that address.

The Aston home was a sprawling brick, traditional, three-story house, tucked privately behind a gated brick wall with loads of perfectly manicured trees and shrubs. There was no way to see into the yard other than sitting right in front of the wrought iron, spear-topped gates, but luck was with Missy. As she turned onto the street that ran in front of the mini-mansion, a candy-apple-red convertible German car, driven by a blonde woman with giant sunglasses and a silk scarf around her neck, pulled out of the drive. The top of the convertible was up for the winter, but even through the lightly tinted glass, Missy caught a good enough glimpse of the driver to be nearly certain that it was indeed Mrs. Aston.

Following a safe distance behind, she trailed the doctor's wife to the country club, where she handed off the keys to a valet. The woman was dressed for tennis, and headed for the indoor courts.

Frustrated that her little adventure had revealed absolutely nothing, Missy started to pull away from her vantage point under some trees near the entrance, when she saw a car with a vanity plate that read, "ATTY SC," pull into the front drive. She wasn't terribly surprised to see Sidney Christianson climb out of the car and hand his keys to the valet, also dressed for tennis.

Hurrying home, she told Chas about that particular 'coincidence,' while taking Toffee for a walk. He listened carefully, scolded her gently about poking around in an investigation, then told her he'd found out some things about Dr. Aston that were worth looking into, promising to fill her in at dinner.

Missy was on pins and needles, waiting for Chas to appear. She had prepared a homemade veggie lasagna that came out absolutely perfectly – the noodles tender, the cheese slightly browned on top, and the slices firm enough to stand on their own without sliding. She opened a full-bodied Cabernet that would be the ultimate complement to the dish, and put crisp, green salads out as an appetizer. The bread sticks that baked in the oven after the lasagna was done were lighter than air and slightly glazed with garlic butter. Her mouth watered at the food, and her heart skipped a beat when she heard Chas's deep voice greeting Toffee in the living room.

She kissed him quickly, suffered impatiently through small talk while they got settled at the dining room table, then started pumping him mercilessly for information.

"So, what did you find out about Dr. Aston?" she asked, tearing the end off of a bread stick and dipping it lightly in her salad dressing.

"I'm fine, thank you, and how was your day?" the detective teased, dark eyes sparkling.

"Chas! You promised that you'd tell me about what you found out at dinner," Missy reminded him. "This…" she said gesturing to the delicious meal in front of them, "…is dinner. Now tell me what you found out," she insisted, spearing a tomato.

Still grinning, Beckett ate a forkful of lasagna, chewed, swallowed, and took a sip of wine before responding, enjoying her impatience. "Okay, okay," he raised his hands in surrender, then sobered. "When I tried to look into Aston's history, I came up with nearly nothing. It was as though he didn't exist prior to about five years ago, so I looked outside the area for what I could find, and some very interesting things came up."

"Like what?" she prompted, sipping her wine.

"Like, his track record for patients dying is very strange. He typically loses two to three a year, and they almost always die the same way, no matter what symptoms they had to begin with," he explained.

"What do you mean?" Missy was mystified.

"Whether they came in for an injury, or an illness, they all followed the same pattern prior to their death. They'd slip into a coma that would last for a couple of weeks, then die of an embolism."

"Wow, that's a strange coincidence," Missy frowned.

"It seems that a medical board in Illinois thought so too. They did a formal investigation of Aston, but never found enough evidence to charge him with anything, so they advised him that he could either resign his position or be fired, and that's how he ended up in Louisiana. Once he got here, the pattern decreased, but one of the deaths makes me really suspicious," Chas commented, lips pursed in thought.

"Suspicious…why?"

"Because his patient was Cheryl's mother."

Missy's mouth dropped open. "What? Are you serious?" she breathed, eyes going wide.

"Deadly serious, but that's not even the most interesting part. Aston was one of the loudest voices calling for Stanley Conner, Cheryl's stepfather, to be prosecuted for the crime."

"Hmm…deflecting attention from himself maybe?" she muttered, eyes narrowed.

"That's what I'm thinking. There was also a time a few years ago where his own wife mysteriously slipped into a coma, but came out of it a couple of weeks later," he added.

"And when you consider that we saw her with another man at lunch today, it makes it entirely possible that she may have been about to become his next victim," Missy's pointed out.

Chas nodded.

"That was my thought. Of course this is all speculation at

this point, but I'm definitely going to be doing more digging to see what I can find out about Dr. Aston. It's a general rule of thumb that you don't investigate doctors when there's a murder, because they've essentially spent their entire lives trying to maintain and extend life rather than ending it, but at the end of the day, they're just people too – people who can, and do, sometimes succumb to evil impulses."

Missy shuddered and she set down her fork.

"Chas, Ben is in a coma, and is in the care of Dr. Aston… what if he's next?"

"Let's not jump to any conclusions. While the evidence that I've found seems to point to Dr. Aston, we have to remember that every time someone was suspicious about him, there was never enough evidence to even charge him. It could be merely a series of bizarre coincidences," he shrugged.

"But it could also be that this guy is just really talented when it comes to covering his tracks, and I really don't want to gamble on that with Ben's life," she exclaimed. "Can't we petition the hospital to get Ben a different doctor because his current one is in the process of suing him?" she pleaded, her heart pounding.

Ben was at the hospital right now, alone and vulnerable, except for the shadow of a fiancée sitting in a chair in the corner.

"I'll see what I can do," Beckett nodded. "And in the mean-time, I hate to say it, but if Aston didn't kill Stanley Conner, Cheryl certainly would have had the motive to do it."

"But if Cheryl killed her stepfather, then who tried to kill Ben by cutting his brake line?" Missy demanded, pointing out the inconsistency.

"Good question, and one that I intend to find the answer to. As for you, young lady, no more following around doctor's wives looking for dirt, understand? If Aston is capable of doing what we think he may have done, you could be unnecessarily putting yourself in danger," he warned.

"Okay," Missy nodded. "It's just so confusing and scary, I hate feeling helpless.

"I know," Chas agreed, sympathetic. "Hopefully, it'll all be over soon."

Chapter 13

Feeling more than a bit nervous walking into the hospital after her strange conversation with Chas, Missy visited Ben's room again the next morning, disturbed, but no longer surprised to see Cheryl in her usual spot in the corner. The shadows kept her mostly hidden from view, but when Missy politely said hello, she could've sworn that the pale, unkempt girl was clutching something in her hands, as if to hide it. Missy went directly to the bed and placed a hand lovingly on Ben's cheek, trying to hold back her tears.

"Oh Ben, honey, please wake up," she pleaded quietly, hoping that somehow, he could hear her.

She searched his face for any sign of movement, any twitch that might give her hope, and found no peace in the smooth, still skin. Wiping her eyes with the back of her hand, Missy heard a soft sound behind her and turned to see Cheryl's shoulders shaking with the force of her tears as she bowed her head and cried. As though feeling Missy's gaze, she slowly raised her head.

"I talk to him every day…just hoping that he'll blink or something, but every day, there's no change," she choked out, overcome. "I wonder if I'll ever hear his sweet voice say my name again, or if I'll ever feel his kiss. It hurts so bad." The bereft young woman clutched at her sides, her head dropping again. At a loss, Missy squeezed her shoulder on the way out, not knowing what to think.

* * *

Finding strength and purpose in her daily routine, Missy went to her LaChance shop after the disconcerting visit, glad to see that Grayson and Chris were still doing well.

"Hey Ms. G.," Grayson greeted her. "How's Ben doing?"

"The same, unfortunately," Missy made a face.

"I ran into Cheryl at the grocery store a couple of nights ago. That girl is messed up," he shook his head sadly.

"Messed up? What do you mean?" Missy tried to sound casual, but concerned.

"Well, you know what she's been like. She doesn't eat, she doesn't sleep, she spends all of her time at the hospital, and when I tried to talk to her, she kept muttering about how it's her duty to watch Ben and protect him from the bad man. It really creeped me out, but I feel bad for her, you know?" the youth shrugged, uncomfortable.

"Of course you do, Grayson, it's just a sad thing all the way around. Did she say who the bad man was?" Missy asked, her heart beating fast.

"No, she was really out of it, so I didn't ask her any questions. Do you think Ben's going to be okay?" he asked, brushing his thick, black hair out of his soulful eyes.

"I hope so Grayson, I really hope so."

Chapter 14

Missy had just selected a movie to watch, when her phone rang, Chas's number popping up on her screen.

"Hey, handsome," she answered with a smile.

"Hey, beautiful," he responded automatically. "I'll be over in a few minutes, with big news," he promised, refusing to elaborate when Missy badgered him with questions.

"What is it?" she pounced on him the moment he entered the door.

"Yes, I'd love a glass of wine, thanks," he raised his eyebrows at her, heading to the powder room to wash his hands and shooing her toward the kitchen. By the time he came out, Missy had two glasses of wine poured and waiting on the coffee table, and the rest of the bottle within easy reach if they should need it. Toffee curled up under the table, happy that both of her favorite people were present.

"Okay, *now*," Missy's curiosity bubbled over. "What is the big news?"

The detective savored a sip of wine. "I had a call from the Smithville PD…" he began.

"Smithville?" Missy interrupted. "That's where Ben said that he ended up on the night of the murder."

"I'm aware," Chas nodded, amused. "So, apparently, the sergeant on duty received a call this afternoon about an abandoned car. One of the locals had gone duck hunting on his land, and stumbled upon a car that got stuck in the swamp. They ran the plates and found out that the car belonged to Stanley Conner. The boys over in Smithville knew that we'd been investigating the murder of Stanley Conner, so they secured a perimeter and called us. My guys went out there and found footprints, hairs in the trunk that look to be a match for Ben's hair, and hairs on the driver's seat that don't look to be a match with Stanley Conner."

"Which means what, exactly?" Missy asked, eyes wide, wondering how close to death Ben had come.

"Well, we figure that whoever killed Stanley, did it in his car, outside of the hotel. Looking for a way to hide the body, they conveniently stumbled upon a man in a clown costume and knocked him out, stealing the costume. Ben was dragged out and stuffed into the trunk, and Stanley was dressed in the costume and staged in the break room, giving the killer time to drive away in Stanley's car. The killer dumped Ben in the park, while he was still unconscious, then drove to the swamp to ditch the car, abandoning it when it got stuck. The footprints around the car had to be those of the killer, aside from the ones made by the duck hunter who found it."

"I knew it! I knew Ben was innocent!" Missy said fiercely, tears of joy in her eyes. "And if it happened the way that you said it did, Cheryl couldn't have done it either, because she wouldn't have been strong enough to drag Ben's body into the trunk or Stanley's body into the hotel."

"Exactly," Chas nodded, impressed with her deduction.

"So now all you have to do is find who the real killer is," she observed.

"Actually, I still need to go over the reports from the lab, but I believe that we've already found the killer," Chas replied.

"Really? How?"

"There was a very thick file folder tucked underneath the liner of the trunk which contained a wealth of extremely incriminating information. As it turns out, Stanley Conner had come to town because he was blackmailing Dr. Bernard Radcliffe Aston," he revealed.

"Blackmailing him? About what?" Missy was astonished.

"Apparently, Stanley knew about Aston's past, and his ability to...eliminate people when necessary. The two had made a pact to kill Cheryl's mother, but, halfway through the process, while she was still in a coma and able to be saved, Stanley got cold feet and tried to talk Aston out of doing it. Aston had tasted the thrill of death before, and nothing was going to deter him from the task at hand. Stanley collected the insurance money and the two agreed to keep the cause of death a secret, but when an investigation began, Aston accused Stanley of the crime, nearly getting him indicted. Stanley held a grudge from that moment forward, and when he ran out of insurance money, he planned to blackmail Aston.

"There were copies of emails between the two, which culminated in a plan to meet at the hotel during the function so that

Aston could pay him off. The autopsy report showed that Stanley was given a lethal injection combined with a sedative, in the left side of his neck and that the needle was at an angle consistent with someone standing outside the car and reaching in to give the injection."

"So, Dr. Aston is a serial killer?" Missy asked, horrified. "I knew I didn't like him."

"So it would seem," Beckett nodded. "While I was going over the evidence, I got a very strange call from Cheryl. I went to the hospital to pick her up, and she refused to leave Ben's room, but she handed me a series of syringes that she had collected from the trash when Aston would leave the room late at night. Bernard Aston had been coming into Ben's room every night to give him a dose of meds that kept him in a chemical coma. The residue in the syringes confirmed that, but even more disturbing was the final syringe," he paused.

"Why? What was in the final syringe?" Missy held her breath.

"Nothing at all. Aston was in the process of squeezing 20ml of air into Ben's IV line in order to cause an embolism, when Cheryl, who had hidden from the nurses and stayed past visiting hours, made a sound, startling him. His hand jumped, causing him to drop the syringe, and he quickly left the room. Cheryl grabbed the syringe, relieved that the doctor hadn't had time to inject hardly any air. When she was sure that he was gone, she called me. After speaking with her, I sent officers in to pick up Aston, and he confessed to everything. He even admitted to giving his daughter the cupcake that put her in the hospital. That's why the empty wrapper was found near Ben's car. Aston wanted it to look like Ben had done it, but in truth, he did it himself while Ben was in the trunk of Stanley's car."

"How awful! How on earth could he do that to his own child?" Missy wondered, appalled.

"Well, as it turns out, she's not actually his child, she was fathered by Sidney Christianson."

"So, we were right about the affair!" Missy breathed, wide-eyed.

Chas nodded. "The important thing is that, now that the hospital staff is aware of what's been going on, they've begun the process of bringing Ben out of his chemically induced coma. By this time tomorrow, he should be talking to you again," the detective grinned.

Missy shot up out of her seat and leaped into his arms. "Oh, thank goodness! Chas, thank you for giving me the best news I've had in a very long time!"

The detective smiled and hugged her back, but then became serious again. "I think there's someone else who could probably use a big hug right now," he said gently, his eyes kind but holding a bit of reproach.

"Cheryl," Missy whispered, suddenly contrite. "I was so mean to that poor child, and all the while she's been lurking in Ben's hospital room after hours, gathering evidence to convict a serial killer. Oh Chas, I feel awful. Why was I so ugly to that girl?" she moaned, her eyes flooding with tears.

"Because you thought she might have killed someone and put your beloved Ben in danger," he reminded her. "But, I'm guessing that an apology would probably do both of you good," he encouraged.

Missy nodded. "You're absolutely right. I'm going down to the hospital now. Do you think she'll be there?"

"I know she'll be there," Chas said confidently. "I arranged for special visiting hours for her, so that she can stay with Ben 24/7 until he's well enough to come home."

"Chas Beckett, you're an amazing man, you know that?" Missy said, leaning her forehead against his.

"Stop it now, you'll make me blush," he teased, kissing her soundly. "Now go get your shoes, and I'll drive you to the hospital.

Chapter 15

Missy poked her head into the door of Ben's hospital room. Today was the day that he was supposed to be fully conscious again, and true to form, he was sitting up in bed, eating a cupcake that Grayson had brought, against doctor's orders. Her entire staff, from both shops, surrounded the bed, and it touched her heart to see all of the people that she considered family there supporting Ben. Seeing Missy in the doorway, he waved her over, his mouth too full of red velvet cupcake to speak. Tears in her eyes, Missy moved as though in slow motion to stand at Ben's bedside. Her dear loyal Ben opened his arms wide, and she moved in for a hug, no words needed. Her tears wet his thin hospital gown, and he didn't mind a bit.

"Hey, Ms. G.," he soothed, after swallowing his massive bite of cupcake. "It's okay, I'm all good now."

She pulled back, drying her eyes with the back of her hand. "I was so worried about you," she confessed. "I don't know what I would've done if you hadn't recovered."

"Well, fortunately I had a stubborn little guardian angel

watching over me from the recliner in the corner," he joked, reaching for Cheryl's hand. "And she's going to need some help planning our wedding, if you don't mind."

"The wedding is back on?" Missy asked, overjoyed at the news. "Oh honey," she said, glancing over at Cheryl. "We have work to do – we've lost so much planning time with all of this murder nonsense." Everyone in the room laughed at the abrupt change of focus, and once again, life was on its way back to normal.

Chapter 16

Cheryl wrung her hands nervously as Missy tucked stray curls back into the bride's elaborate up-do on a beautiful Spring morning.

"You, my dear, are just a perfect vision," Missy proclaimed, gazing at the bride, who was beautiful from head to toe.

"Thank you so much, Ms. G., I couldn't have done this without you," she replied, tears welling in her beautiful blue eyes.

"Oh no, darlin, don't do that!" Missy exclaimed, jumping up to fan the girl's face, and dabbing at her with a tissue. "Your mascara will run."

"I don't care," the lovely young woman whispered, reaching for Missy's hand. "I want you to know how much you mean to me, and to Ben. Neither of us has our mom anymore, but believe me when I tell you…we both think of you as our new mom. You're always there for us, and we know that we can count on you, no matter what," her lower lip trembled, but when she smiled, her eyes shone with love.

"Oh, honey, now you're making me cry," Missy laughed and hugged her lightly, being careful not to crush the top of her gown. "I love you two with all my heart, and I love it that I get to marry off my son and my daughter on the same day," she beamed proudly.

Just then a heart-stoppingly handsome Chas Beckett, fully decked out in a tuxedo because he had the honor of escorting Cheryl to the altar, knocked softly on the bedroom door. Ben and Cheryl were getting married in the gazebo in Missy's spacious backyard, and it was nearly time for the lovely bride's entrance.

"Are we ready?" he asked, bowing and offering his arm.

Both ladies nodded, brushing away tears. Missy kissed Cheryl's cheek and headed down to check on Ben, who was waiting to get in place before the arrival of his bride.

"Hey, darlin," Missy greeted him with a hug. "You ready for this?" she teased.

"More ready than I've ever been for anything," he confessed, blushing.

"Y'all are going to be so happy. I'm proud of you, Ben. You're one of the most amazing men I know," she pinched his cheek fondly.

"And maybe one of the others will be putting you through all of this sometime soon," he waggled his eyebrows at her, teasing.

"Get on up to that altar, young man," Missy grinned, kissing his cheek. "Your bride will be down here any minute." She practically floated to her seat in the front row, her sage-green chiffon dress billowing gracefully around her.

A lively piece of classical music began, and Ben filed in with Grayson and Chris to stand at the altar in the gazebo. Bridesmaids were not necessary, as Grayson stood on Cheryl's side. The sweet, quiet youth was her best friend, and the only attendant that she would accept. Toffee was the ring-bearer, and wagged her tail wildly, prancing proudly down the aisle to stand with Ben. The music changed, and all the guests stood and turned as the first strains of the bridal march began to play.

Missy's heart was in her throat as she witnessed the precious picture made by the angelic bride, and her handsome escort. Tears sprung to her eyes as they made their way, formally in step, down the aisle. She couldn't help but wonder how it must feel to be in Cheryl's shoes, making your way to your soon-to-be-mate, promising him an eternity of life, laughter and love. She'd always shied away from the idea of marriage, but the serenity and joy in the faces of Ben and Cheryl made her wonder, if only for a moment, about the wisdom of her choice.

Her glance moved to Chas Beckett, the most handsome man in the room, or in the world, as far as Missy was concerned. How would it feel to walk down the aisle knowing that he would be waiting for her, hand outstretched, at the end? A sudden warmth swept through her, from her head to her toes, as she realized, powerfully, irrevocably, that she was in love with Detective Chas Beckett, and in this moment, should he have chosen to let go of the bride and take her hand instead, she would have followed him to the altar, or to the ends of the earth.

Chapter 17

Ben and Cheryl's wedding had been a touching, warm, heart-felt affair that had everyone dabbing at their eyes while smil-ing. The love between the newlyweds was an alive, nearly tangible thing that moved anyone who was lucky enough to witness it. While Missy's backyard was large enough for the ceremony, the reception was being held, ironically enough, in the grand hotel where Ben had been rendered unconscious and stuffed in a trunk. The event was catered, but the couple had insisted that, instead of a traditional wedding cake, they had to have a "cake" made of just over one hundred and fifty of their favorite cupcakes. The entire staff had made an event of baking the 'cake' the day before, with a cupcake extrava-ganza at the LaChance shop, fueled by pizza, beer and fun and supervised by stand-in father-of-the-bride, Chas.

Chas danced with Cheryl for the father-daughter dance, and Missy danced with Ben for the mother-son dance, with Grayson catching the garter and 90-year-old Mildred Feldman catching the bouquet. The evening was filled with laughter and dancing, and Missy was delighted to find that her tall-dark-and-handsome boyfriend certainly knew what to do on the dance floor. After a rigorous combination of 80's dance tunes, she and the detective plopped down happily at a table next to the dance floor for some rest and refreshment.

Caught up in the sweetness of the moment, Missy gazed out at the dancers with a smile lighting her face. "What a perfectly wonderful day," she sighed, taking Chas's hand.

"Mmm…" he nodded, brushing her cheek with a kiss. "I never thought about this stage of life, getting married, that kind of thing, but it's pretty amazing to see it happening right in front of me, to two people that I care about," he mused.

"I know exactly what you mean," Missy nodded. "I found myself thinking about things differently today, as though a whole world that I'd never considered before could actually be a possibility."

"I'm surprised that you've never been married," Chas admitted. "How is it that no Prince Charming ever swept you off of your feet and put a ring on that elegant finger?" he asked, kissing her hand.

"Well, I took over running the store, while going to school, when my parents died, and that basically set the course for my life. I've dedicated myself to running my shop since I was 17, and just never had the time or inclination to commit entirely to a relationship," she shrugged.

"And now?" he asked, his eyes holding her captive.

Missy's heart pounded as she weighed the possibilities of just how honest she was willing to be. Ultimately, she trusted

Chas Beckett, and if her feelings for him scared him away, it would be better to find out sooner rather than later, so she opted for honesty. "And now…I can see more possibilities than I could before," she swallowed hard, wondering how he'd react. She'd never shared her feelings quite so intimately with anyone before, this was scary territory.

"Meaning?" he prodded, encouraging her to share how she felt.

"Meaning that…" she began.

"Hey you two! Why so serious over here?" Mayor Felton Chadwick boisterously interrupted the intimate moment. "It's a party – time to eat, drink and be merry!" he patted his generous tummy looking like he'd been indulging in two of the three at the very least. "Miss Gladstone, may I request the pleasure of your company on the dance floor?" he held out a pudgy hand.

"I…uh…" Missy was at a loss, still not having recovered from nearly telling Chas exactly how she felt about him.

"That's a great idea, sweetie," Chas helped her out. "Go have your dance with Mr. Mayor, and I'll meet you back here with a gin and tonic, sound good?" he grinned conspiratorially.

Relieved at having been eased back into reality, Missy nodded gratefully, taking the Mayor's hand while Chas headed toward the bar.

Despite his considerable size, Mayor Chadwick was quite the graceful dancer, much to Missy's surprise. As he skillfully whirled and twirled her about, she learned the real reason for his dance invitation.

"Now Miss Gladstone, I have to say, you've outdone yourself with this lovely reception. Not only were those wedding cupcakes heavenly, but everything from the set-up to the food selection and the décor is just absolutely perfect. I don't know if you're aware, but my lovely daughter, Priscilla is getting married next year. Her sweet mama, bless her soul, is a lovely woman of good character and refinement, but the poor dear can't plan an event to save her life. I don't even want to get into the fiasco that occurred when my dear Prissy graduated from high school," he shook his head in disgust. "My question to you is this…would you be willing, for the right price of course, to help my Priscilla plan her wedding? It would mean so much to my family," he smiled, anticipating a yes. Mayor Chadwick was a man who was not accustomed to being turned down.

"Oh, Mayor Chadwick, I'm flattered, but I'm not a wedding planner. I helped out Cheryl because she has no family to speak of, but this isn't something with which I have a whole lot of experience," Missy answered honestly.

"You know my dear, I've often found that sometimes the things that we're really good at, take us by surprise when we're not even looking for them. You clearly have a gift for this sort of work, maybe it's something that you should consider doing. In this particular case, I'd make the effort more than worth your time. My little princess is getting married, and I swear to you, her wedding will be the biggest and best that this parish has ever seen. If you make that happen, little lady, you can write your own ticket. You think about it and you let me know," he smiled at her benevolently.

Missy was speechless. "Umm…okay, Mr. Mayor. I'll let you know."

"Darlin, there's no need for such formality among friends, please, call me Felton. I'll look forward to hearing from you," he said, bowing and kissing her hand as the song ended, then leading her back to where Chas mercifully waited with a tall, icy, gin and tonic.

"What was that all about?" Chas grinned at her, having noticed her discomfort on the dance floor as she considered the mayor's proposition.

She told him what Chadwick had proposed, and that she had tried to demur.

The detective swirled the ice cubes in his glass. "Felton Chadwick is not a man who takes no for an answer, you realize that, right?" he asked.

"Yeah, I definitely picked up on that vibe," Missy agreed, taking a sip of her crisp, bubbly drink and letting it soothe her.

"So, what would be so terrible about doing it?" Chas asked reasonably. "You'd make a ridiculous amount of money, because that man doesn't believe in doing anything cheaply, you'd be doing something you enjoy that showcases your talent, and who knows…it could be yet another business pursuit for you. Besides, it'd be good practice for you if you ever need to plan your own wedding someday," he added with a faint smile.

"Like that would ever happen," Missy laughed softly at the thought.

"Who knows what the future may bring?" the detective remarked enigmatically, draining his glass. "I'm getting a refill," he said, standing. "Would you like anything?"

"No, I'm good," Missy murmured, unable to look away from the stunning man in front of her. When he kissed her cheek before heading to the bar, she raised her hand to the spot where his lips had been, emotions flooding her with a fear-tinged delight.

Chapter 18

Missy had closed the Dellville shop for a week while Ben and Cheryl were on their honeymoon, so that Grayson and Chris could both work at the LaChance shop. Business at Missy's Frosted Love Cupcakes had picked back up once it was proved that neither Missy nor Ben had made Dr. Aston's daughter sick by giving her the wrong cupcake. Loretta Christianson had personally stopped by to apologize for being rude to Missy and had made phone calls to her society friends who were having events, encouraging them to patronize the shop. She had confided to Missy that she knew her husband had fathered Mrs. Aston's child, but that she chose to look the other way because she and Sidney were unable to have children. Missy felt nothing but pity and admiration for the childless socialite who devoted herself to serving her community, and had forgiven her entirely for the mistreatment that she had suffered.

Missy was happily creating a new Cupcake of the Day in her spotless commercial kitchen, when Grayson came back to speak with her, eyes wide.

"Ms. G.," he whispered, clearly excited about something. "You'll never guess who's up front, wanting to talk to you."

Setting down her measuring cup, Missy smiled, intrigued. "Who might that be, Grayson?"

"The Mayor! Mayor Chadwick is here, and he wants to talk to you," the youth exclaimed, still whispering and clearly awed.

Missy was amused. "Well, send him back, I'm right in the middle of a new recipe," she directed.

"Yes ma'am," Grayson disappeared in a flash.

"Good morning!" Felton Chadwick's voice boomed when he strolled into the kitchen, resplendent in a navy blue suit with a red vest and tie. "How are you on this fine Louisiana morning, little lady?"

"I'm well, thank you Felton, and you?" Missy asked, measuring cups of flour and dumping them into a bowl.

"Just dandy," he grinned, coming over to peer in the bowl. "What's this fine creation?" he asked, unconsciously rubbing his ample stomach.

"I'm creating a new recipe, and calling it Boston Cream Cupcakes. They'll be like miniature Boston Cream Pies, with a yellow cupcake, filled with vanilla pudding and topped with fudge frosting," she explained, much to the Mayor's delight.

His stomach growled audibly, and Missy giggled, plucking a Coconut Cream Cupcake from a nearby tray and handing it to him. "Here, try one of these, I think you'll like it, and you can grab a cup of coffee over there," she gestured to the coffee maker burbling happily in the corner as it finished brewing a fresh pot. "That one is for staff only, we like having our own supply," she explained, cracking some eggs into her bowl.

"Well, my stars, Missy Gladstone, this is quite the setup you have here," Chadwick nodded appreciatively, taking a large bite of his cupcake and pouring a steaming mug of fresh coffee.

"It's humble, but it's home," Missy smiled proudly. She loved her thriving little shop, and delighted in seeing others react positively to her efforts.

"Well now, darlin, the reason I popped in to see you today, other than making a shameless ploy to procure some of your baked goods, is to ask you what your thoughts are concerning my Priscilla's wedding," he looked at her pointedly, but with his same glad-handing politician's smile.

"I've thought about it," Missy stopped stirring for a moment. "And I've decided that, as a favor to you, and to help out your lovely wife, I'd be happy to take on the planning of your daughter's wedding," she smiled, breaking the happy news.

"I knew I could count on you," Chadwick beamed, pleased with himself. "You just let me know how much you're going to charge for your services, and don't be shy young lady, money is no object. You just make sure that what my Prissy wants, she gets, ya hear?"

"I will do my best, Felton," Missy nodded. "When do I get to meet her?"

"I'll have my wife arrange a luncheon for the three of you at my house, she's capable of doing that much," he joked, fanning himself. "Then you and Prissy can get together and talk about all of those girly details that mystify me."

"That sounds lovely, I'll look forward to it," she smiled, carefully pouring batter into pre-arranged foil cups.

"Well, that's settled then," the Mayor clapped his hands together, having finished his cupcake in three bites. He took another swig of coffee, then set his mug in one of the stainless-steel sinks. "I surely do appreciate this, Missy Gladstone. Just…one more thing…" he trailed off as though uncertain how to phrase what he wanted to say.

"Yes?" Missy inquired.

"My Prissy…well, some folks find her a bit…opinionated," he shrugged.

Missy nodded and smiled. "Not a problem, Felton," she assured him. "She's the bride. It's her day, and we'll make sure that she gets exactly what she wants."

Chadwick chuckled nervously and nodded. "Well, that's good then. That's what she's accustomed to."

He said his goodbyes and Missy watched him go, shaking her head. What could possibly be so difficult about figuring out what Priscilla Chadwick wanted and making it happen? Men were so silly sometimes. She put her Boston Cream Cupcakes in the preheated oven to bake, and leaned back against the counter, thinking about the past few weeks.

A murder had been solved, Ben and Cheryl had gotten married, she'd been drafted as a wedding planner, and Chas had been looking at her in a new way that made her heart skip a beat whenever he was around. Life was good in LaChance, Louisiana. Missy couldn't wait to tell her friend Echo, who owned the vegan ice cream shop in Dellville, all about it when the free-spirited former Californian returned from her vacation in India. Smiling to herself, she took off her apron and headed back to the front, confident in knowing that all was right with her world.

Did you enjoy this story? Check out book 9 in the series today!

Honey Dripped Murder

Teddy Bear Cupcakes

Cupcakes

1 1/2 cups All-Purpose flour

2 Tbsp corn starch

1/2 cup unsweetened cocoa powder

2 tsp baking powder

1 cup powdered sugar

1 1/2 sticks of butter (room temperature)

1 cup sugar

2 eggs (room temperature)

½ cup plain yogurt

¼ cup milk

1 tsp vanilla extract

Beat butter and sugar until fluffy.

Add eggs one at a time until pale yellow in color.

Add vanilla extract, plain yogurt, and milk.

Add flour, powdered sugar, unsweetened cocoa powder, baking powder, corn starch. Mix well, sift.

Bake at 350 degrees for about 15-18 minutes.

Chocolate Butter Frosting

1/2 stick of butter (room temperature)

1/3 cup unsweetened cocoa powder

2 cups powdered sugar

1 tsp vanilla extract

1/4 cup milk

Beat butter and sugar together until creamy. Slowly add in powdered sugar, unsweetened cocoa powder, milk and vanilla extract. Mix until desired consistency.

Vanilla butter frosting

1/2 stick of butter (room temperature)

2 cups powdered sugar

1 tsp vanilla extract

2 Tbsp milk

Beat butter, sugar, vanilla, and milk until soft peaks form.

Frost cupcakes when they are cool.

About the Author

Summer Prescott is a USA Today and Wall Street Journal Best-Selling Author, who has penned nearly one hundred Cozy Mysteries, and one rather successful Thriller, The Quiet Type, which debuted in the top 50 of its genre. As owner of Summer Prescott Books Publishing, Summer is responsible for a combined catalog of over two hundred Cozy Mysteries and Thrillers. Mentoring and helping new Cozy writers launch their careers has long been a passion of Summer's, and she has played a key role in the incredible success of Cozy writers such as Patti Benning and Carolyn Q. Hunter.

Summer enjoys travel, and is honored to be a featured speaker at the International Writer's Conference in Cuenca, Ecuador, in May 2018. The event draws writers from all over the world.

In an exciting development, Summer has recently been asked to write monthly for her favorite magazine, Atomic Ranch. Having been an Interior Decorator before giving up her business to write full-time, Summer is thrilled by the opportunity and looking forward to having her writing published in the only magazine to which she actually subscribes.

Summer is a doting mother to four grown children, and lives in Champaign, Illinois with her Standard Poodle, Elvis.

Author's Note

I'd love to hear your thoughts on my books, the storylines, and anything else that you'd like to comment on—reader feedback is very important to me. My contact information, along with some other helpful links, is listed on the next page. If you'd like to be on my list of "folks to contact" with updates, release and sales notifications, etc.... just shoot me an email and let me know. Thanks for reading!

Also…

… if you're looking for more great reads, Summer Prescott Books publishes several popular series by outstanding Cozy Mystery authors.

Contact Summer Prescott

Website http://summerprescottbooks.com

Email: summer.prescott.cozies@gmail.com

Newsletter: Sign Up

And…be sure to check out the Summer Prescott Cozy Mysteries fan page and Summer Prescott Books Publishing Page on Facebook – let's be friends!

Made in the USA
Columbia, SC
17 July 2021

41979950R10064